LOOK AND FIND®

SPACE CHIMPS

Illustrated by Art Mawhinney
Written by Caleb Burroughs

Space Chimps™ & © 2008 Vanguard Animation, LLC
All rights reserved.

Published by Louis Weber, C.E.O.
Publications International, Ltd.
7373 North Cicero Avenue, Lincolnwood, Illinois 60712
Ground Floor, 59 Gloucester Place, London W1U 8JJ

Customer Service: 1-800-595-8484 or customer_service@pilbooks.com

www.pilbooks.com

Manufactured in China.

p i kids is a registered trademark of Publications International, Ltd.
Look and Find is a registered trademark of Publications International, Ltd.,
in the United States and in Canada.

8 7 6 5 4 3 2 1

ISBN-13: 978-1-4127-7457-4
ISBN-10: 1-4127-7457-8

Ladies and gentlemen, strap yourselves in as we embark on a mission to the stars. Flying through the air tonight for your enjoyment will be Ham, the space chimp! As Ham prepares to blast off, find these other entertaining circus acts.

This clown

Bird girl

Escape artist

Bearded lady

Ringmaster

Siamese twins

Girl on the flying trapeze

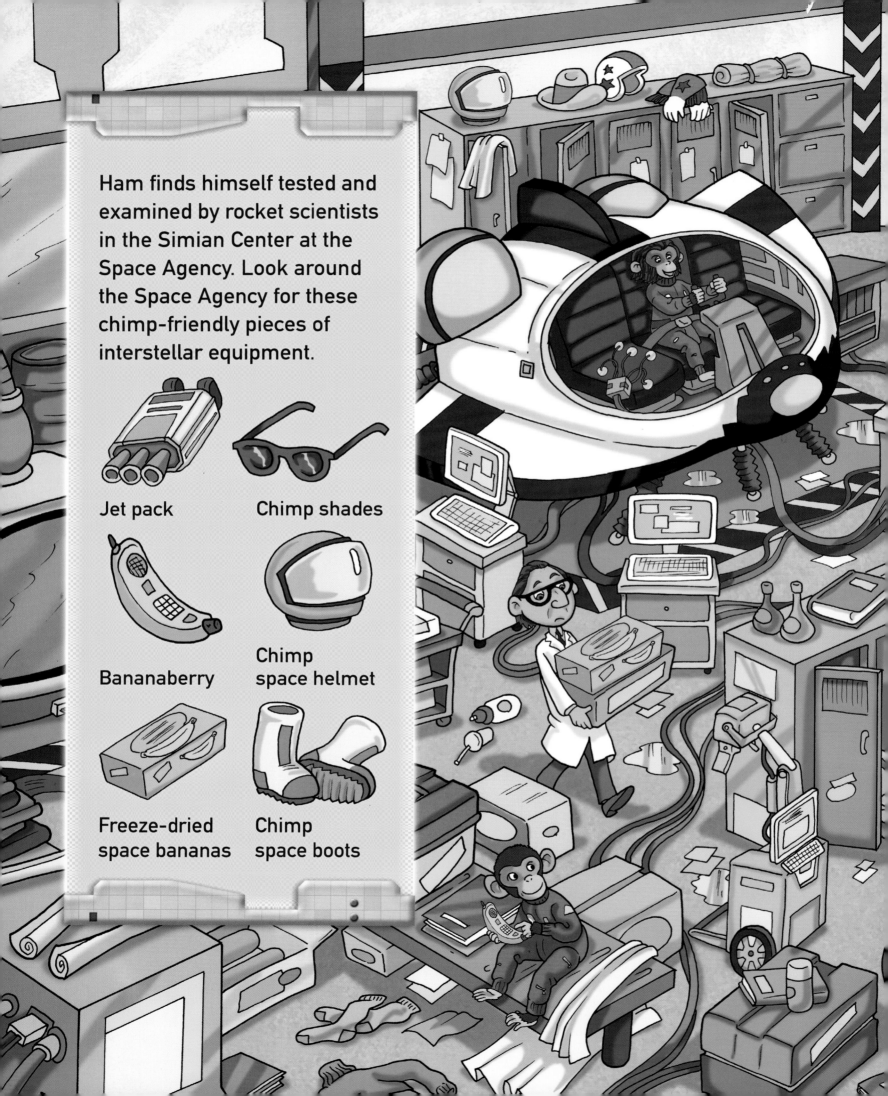

Ham finds himself tested and examined by rocket scientists in the Simian Center at the Space Agency. Look around the Space Agency for these chimp-friendly pieces of interstellar equipment.

Jet pack

Chimp shades

Bananaberry

Chimp space helmet

Freeze-dried space bananas

Chimp space boots

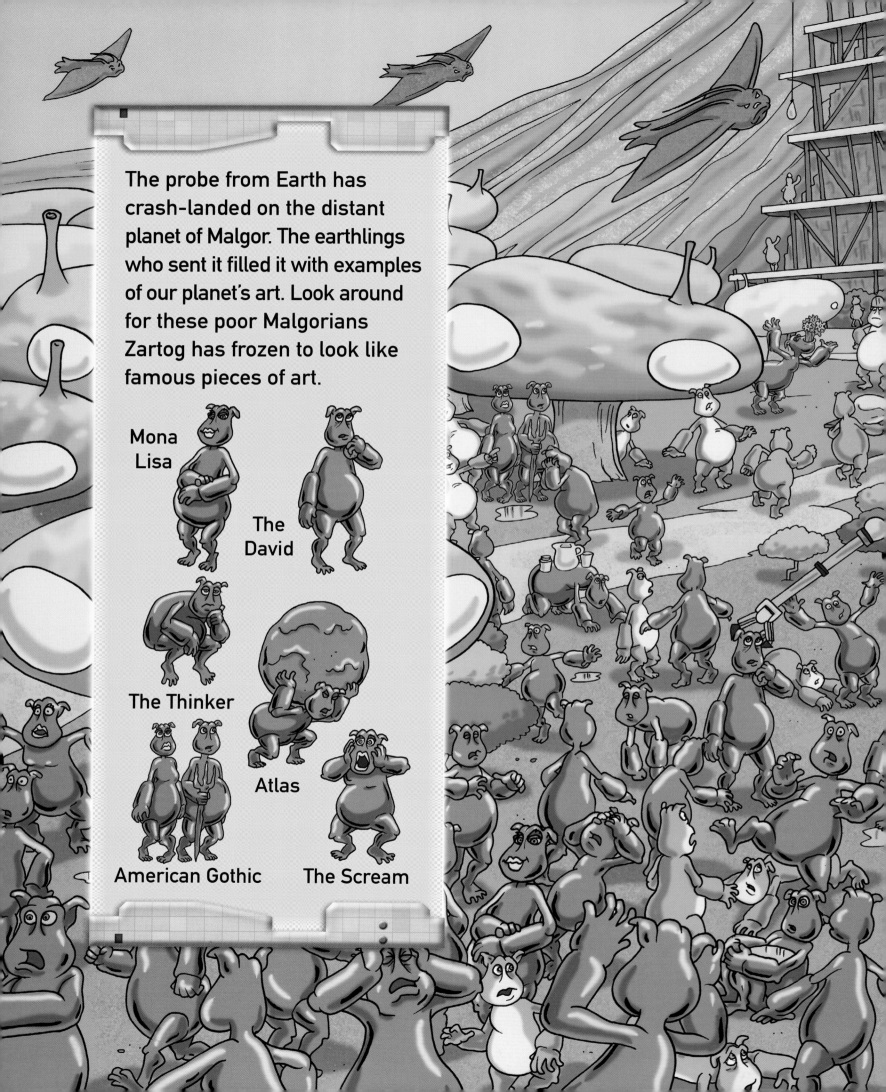

The probe from Earth has crash-landed on the distant planet of Malgor. The earthlings who sent it filled it with examples of our planet's art. Look around for these poor Malgorians Zartog has frozen to look like famous pieces of art.

Mona Lisa

The David

The Thinker

Atlas

American Gothic

The Scream

Ham and Luna crash-land on the alien planet of Malgor. Now they have to escape the alien army—and many other things that want to get them. Swing along with our two heroes and find these dangers that they face.

Splork

Living vine

Malgorian soldier's spear

Quicksand

Snake creature

This Fluvian fighter

The crashed spaceship has been found and carried to Zartog's palace—with Titan still inside! He wakes up to see the strange, new things native to the planet Malgor. See if you can find these alien items.

Alien pie

Lemonslort

Gork Humor truck

Glecknard

Clocce orb

Snizzlefruit

Aboard their homemade spacecraft, The Chimpfinity, our heroes are blasted back home by a volcanic explosion. The grateful inhabitants of Malgor bid them farewell. Try to find these Malgorians that the Space Chimps met.

This alien kid

This Malgorian soldier

Gumdrop aliens

This member of Malgor's marching band

Kilowatt

This Fluvian

With Luna and Titan fast asleep, Ham must pilot the Chimpfinity back to Earth. As he flies through the wormhole, look for these space spots that zoom past.

Halley's Comet

Taurus

Earth

Jupiter

Big Dipper

Orion

Saturn

Welcome home, Space Chimps! Just like Titan always wanted, our primate heroes have been thrown a ticker-tape parade in New York City. Peek around the parade for these things greeting our brave astronauts.

A flag

The chimps on TV

Chimps Rule! banner

A Ham balloon

A Titan balloon

A Luna poster

Launch yourself back to the big top to find these scrumptious circus confections.

Sneak back into the Space Agency to find these tools the scientists use to do their jobs.

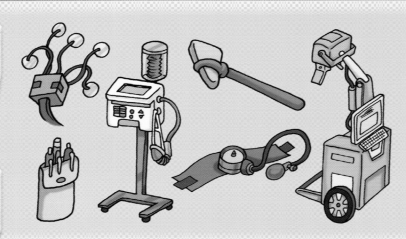

Fly back to Malgor and look for these frozen aliens who the evil Zartog has turned into everyday items.

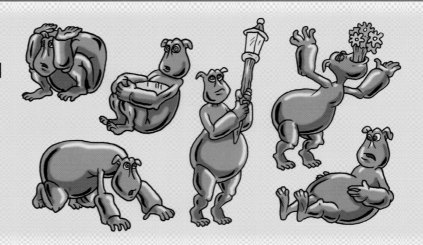

Swing back to Malgor and find some of the things that fell out of Ham's pockets as he tried to escape the alien army.

Go back to Zartog's palace and help Titan tag these Malgorians Organisms 1 through 6.

Blast back to Malgor and look for these things like the ones used to build the Chimpfinity.

Rocket back to the wormhole and look for these pieces of space junk.

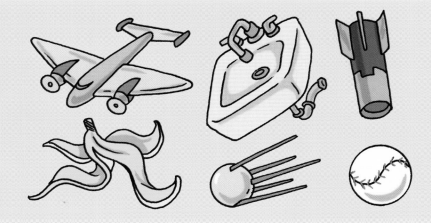

March back through the streets of New York City to find nine bananas scattered around the parade.